To Lindsay, dear friend and dancer
& Tiffany, dear friend and poet
—K. G.

For my beautiful ballerina, Beni!
—S. M.

BEDTIME BALLET

By **Kallie George**   Pictures by **Shanda McCloskey**

L **B**

Little, Brown and Company
New York Boston

Swoosh!

Blue-sky curtain
lifts up and away.
It's time to begin
the Bedtime Ballet.

Back in the shadows,
two wait for their cue,
eager to make
their ballet *debut*.

Two satin slippers
with bunny-ear toes
and stripy pajamas
are dreamy dance clothes.

Daylight dims down
and stars twinkle on.
Fireflies cluster
to spotlight the lawn.

Crickets CHIRRUP
and owls HOO-HOOO low.
The orchestra's ready
so one, two, three . . . go!

A troupe of crisp leaves
chassé 'cross the ground.

Seeds in white tutus
pirouette round.

Flowers raise petals,
with poise, to the sky.

Birds *pas de deux,*
then nestle up high.

Swoosh! goes the curtain. The dance moves inside. The two eager dancers gracefully glide.

Glissé down the hall,
stop at the sink,

relevé to reach
for a brush and a drink.

Kitty jumps close
with a *grand pas de chat*.
Puppy just watches.
His tail thumps to clap.

Plié to kiss
Mama on the cheek.

Battement to brother
who's taking a peek.

A swift lift from Papa,
up over his head,

then a carry upstairs
and a bow into bed.

Bouquets of roses,
pink, red, and white.
"Brava, little dancers.
Brava and good night."

GLOSSARY OF BALLET TERMS

Battement [bat-MAHN]: kicking movement of an extended or bent leg

Chassé [sha-SAY]: sliding movement forward

Debut [dei-byoo]: dancer's first appearance in a performance

Glissé [glee-SAY]: traveling step

Grand pas de chat [grahn pah duh shah]: traveling-sideways jump

Jeté [zhuh-TAY]: jump

Pas de deux [pah duh duh]: duet dance

Pirouette [peer-WET]: whirl or spin

Plié [plee-AY]: smooth bending of the knees, while the upper body is upright

Relevé [ruhl-VAY]: rising onto the toes